FRANCIE & FITZ

BOOSTER BUDDIES

Written by Jenny Harty, CPST

Illustrated By Ellie Beykzadeh

From Our Family to Yours

We're honored to share *Francie & Fitz Booster Buddies* as a gift for your family. This gentle story helps children learn about booster seat safety and, most importantly, can help save lives.

Since 1984, our mission has been simple: to protect families by standing strong for those hurt in accidents, while working hard to prevent injuries before they happen. We hope this book sparks meaningful conversations with your children and helps protect them on every journey.

With warm regards,
David Montlick and the entire Montlick Team

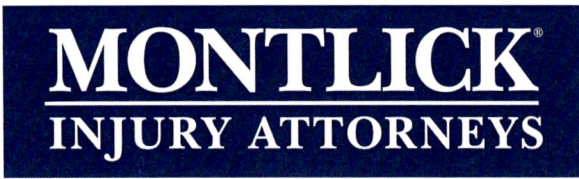

To my daughters who always inspire me to follow my heart — I love you.
To my family and friends who believe and encourage me to chase my dreams — thank you.
And to all my readers and little riders may you always be safe!

About The Author

On July 1, 2002, Jenny Harty and her family were traveling along a rural, two-lane road to visit friends at Lake Sinclair, Georgia, when an accident changed their lives forever. A logging truck ran a stop sign, causing a violent crash that sent their minivan into a deep ravine. Thankfully, Jenny and her family survived, but first responders and doctors all agreed that Madison, Jenny's five-year-old daughter, was saved by the booster seat she was using.

This experience inspired Jenny to take action. Shocked to learn that Georgia's laws didn't require children to use booster seats, she made it her mission to change that. With the support of fellow advocates, she worked tirelessly at the Georgia State Capitol to pass "Madison's Booster Seat Law," which now requires all children under the age of eight to ride in a booster seat or car seat appropriate for their age and height. Jenny's love for her children inspired a powerful drive to keep all children safe on Georgia's roads.

Jenny's commitment to highway safety hasn't stopped there. As a certified National Child Passenger Safety Technician (CPST), she continues to work on important safety initiatives, including helping pass Georgia's "Hands-Free Law" in 2018. For Jenny, this mission is personal: "There are no mulligans, no second chances, when it comes to surviving a car crash." That's why she's dedicated to giving every child the fighting chance they deserve.

Francie & Fitz Booster Buddies is a heartfelt story sent with love to families, with the goal of saving lives and preventing injuries by promoting child passenger safety. According to the Center for Disease Control (CDC), properly securing children in age and size appropriate car seats, booster seats, and seat belts reduces injuries and death by up to 80 percent. Additionally, the CDC recommends children remain in the back seat and properly buckled until at least thirteen years old. Parents and caregivers can make a lifesaving difference by ensuring their children are safely buckled in the back seat on every trip.

It started one steamy hot day in July,
As summer arrived in the blink of an eye,

When Mother smiled warmly and leaned down to say,
"Go outside please, Francie. Find Fitz, and go play!"

Snatching my toy bucket up off of the floor,
I flew down the stairs and pushed open the door.

I ran through the yard, with the sun shining bright,
Off to my friend's house, next door on my right.

I knocked and I knocked, and Fitz promptly appeared,
With big smiles and grins, we both loudly cheered!

Best friends from the start, yes, we just seemed to click,
It happened so smoothly and lickety-split.

With no hesitation, I asked him to play,
"Oh, yes," he responded, "I'd love that today."

Excited we were to begin having fun,
The two of us laughed and we started to run.

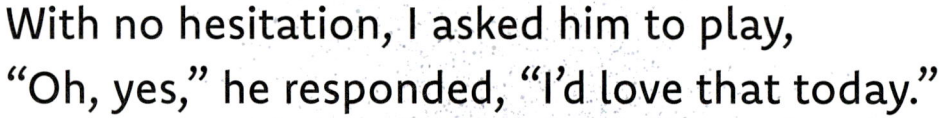

We raced through the sprinklers, played catch in the grass,
Rode bikes and sipped pink lemonade by the glass.

But frisbee was our very favorite to play,
We'd happily throw and catch frisbees all day!

Mom opened the door, and she poked her head out,
"Please come home now, sweetheart!" I heard my mom shout.

"You're having such fun, which is lovely to see,
But we must get going; it's quarter past three."

"Our friends are expecting us down by the lake,
I've packed up the van and baked goodies to take."

I begged my dear mom, "Can Fitz come along too? We'll both be polite and good listeners for you."

Mom furrowed her brow as she tilted her head,
"Hmmm . . . I just don't know, dear," my mother then said.

Fitz melted Mom's heart with his great big, brown eyes,
I smiled till my mouth stretched to three times its size,

Until she said, "Yes, Fitz can join in the fun,
Let's go ask his parents, he's welcome to come."

We hopped in the van, and went to the backseat,
Directly I jumped in my blue booster seat.

Fitz followed behind me, and looked all around,
Paused for a moment, and just sat himself down.

He reached for his seat belt and thought we could go,
"No, wait!" I exclaimed. "Fitz, you're precious cargo."

"We're too small for seat belts alone, Fitz," I cried.
My heart skipped a beat—I explained clearly why.

"We've outgrown our car seats, there is no question,
Booster seats are next, for our best protection."

"It's super important and you need to know,
Booster seats help keep us safe as we still grow.

We get a boost up so the seat belt will fit.
It's much comfier too, I think you'll admit."

His eyes very focused, Fitz nodded his head.
And paid close attention to each word I said.

He thought for a minute, then hung his head low.
He'd been so unsafe, but he just didn't know.

Then quickly I said, "There's no need to be sad,
You've learned a great lesson, for that please be glad."

"When I sit in my booster, I look out and see,
The world all around me, and places I'll be!"

I said to my friend Fitz, "Please lend me your ear,
There's one more important fact you need to hear."

"Under your arm is not where the seat belt sits,
Across your chest, is where it properly fits."

For when seats are buckled and fitting just right,
We're then riding safely, by day and by night."

Fitz shared from his heart, "This is ever so neat! From now on this booster's my new favorite seat!"

We are friends tried and true, the best there could be,
We had so much fun, yelling, "High five! Yippee!"

Then Mom shared a thought, "Believe this, it is true,
You're both precious gifts and we can't replace you!"

We buckled our boosters, we made no mistake,
As loudly I shouted, "Let's go to the lake!"

BOOST YOUR CHILD'S BOOSTER SEAT KNOWLEDGE

- Have your child point to their shoulder bone, chest bone and hip bones, and ask, "What do they feel like to touch?" Typically, a child will say they feel hard like a rock. YES! These bones are very hard and strong.
- Next, have your child point to their tummy and ask what it feels like. Their answer might be that it's soft and squishy like a marshmallow. EXACTLY! Explain to your child that our soft organs are located inside our tummies: our kidneys, liver, stomach, bladder etc.
- Ask your child, "Where do you think the best place for a seat belt would be to keep you safe? On the hard and strong parts of your body, or on your soft and squishy tummy?"
- Discuss with your child how a booster seat works by properly positioning the vehicle's seat belt across the strongest points of the child's body. The lap should be positioned low and across the child's hips, touching the upper thighs—never across the abdomen. The shoulder belt should be across the child's chest, contacting the child's shoulder.

PROPER FITS . . .

- Booster seats should be used for children who have outgrown their harnessed car seat until they are big enough and mature enough to fit and use a seat belt correctly. Remember, seat belts are made for adults.
- Select a booster seat appropriate for the child's age, weight, height, and developmental level.
- When installing a booster seat, ALWAYS read the manufacturer instruction manual for your seat and your vehicle owner's manual.
- The raised seating surface of a booster seat lets the child bend their knees over the booster seat, which keeps the lap belt snug across the child's hips and upper thighs and the shoulder belt across their chest.
- Booster seats are designed to be used with a lap-and-shoulder belt. NEVER use a booster seat with a lap-only belt.
- It is extremely dangerous for children to put the shoulder belt under their arm or behind them. It removes the upper body protection provided by a correctly used seat belt.
- Children should travel in a booster seat until they correctly fit in a seat belt. Children should continue to ride in the back seat.

. . . AND SAFETY TIPS

- It's important to select the right seat and use it correctly every time, including carpools and rideshare services.
- Expiration dates vary between manufacturers. Expiration dates can be found stamped in the shell, on a label, or in the instruction manual. NEVER use an expired car seat or booster seat.
- Following a motor vehicle crash, car seats and booster seats in the vehicle may need to be replaced. Replacement is dependent on the severity of the crash as well as the car seat manufacturer guidelines.
- Register your car seat and booster seat to be notified of important recalls and safety updates by the manufacturer. To do this, visit the manufacturer's website or send in the registration card that came with your car seat or booster seat.
- Children under thirteen years of age should ride in the back seat.
- Booster and child seat laws vary by state. Visit ghsa.org for statewide laws related to child passenger safety.

FOR MORE INFORMATION, PLEASE VISIT:

- *nhtsa.org*
- *ghsa.org*
- *National Child Passenger Safety Board. (2024). Child Passenger Safety Technician Certification Training. National Safety Council. https://www.cpsboard.org/trainings/*
- *National Highway Traffic Safety Administration. (2020). Child Passenger Safety Technician Certification Training. Washington, D.C. https://cdn.nsc.org/psboard/ Technician Guide 2020.pdf*

Written by: Jenny Harty
Illustrated by: Ellie Beykzadeh

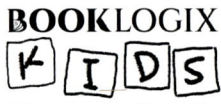

Alpharetta, Georgia

Copyright © 2025 by Jenny Harty
Illustrations Copyright © 2025 by Ellie Beykzadeh

All rights reserved. No part of this book may be reproduced or transmitted in any form or by any means, electronic or mechanical, including photocopying, recording, or any information storage and retrieval system, without permission in writing from the author.

ISBN: 978-1-6653-1015-4 - Softcover
ISBN: 978-1-6653-1016-1 - Hardcover

These ISBNs are the property of BookLogix for the express purpose of sales and distribution of this title. The content of this book is the property of the copyright holder only. BookLogix does not hold any ownership of the content of this book and is not liable in any way for the materials contained within. The views and opinions expressed in this book are the property of the Author/Copyright holder, and do not necessarily reflect those of BookLogix.

Library of Congress Control Number: 2025905565

☺ This paper meets the requirements of ANSI/NISO Z39.48-1992 (Permanence of Paper)

0 4 0 8 2 5

Francie & Fitz Booster Buddies

CONNECT WITH US
francieandfitz.com
jen@francieandfitz.com

FOLLOW US ON INSTAGRAM AND FACEBOOK
@francieandfitz